To:

Taryn

Big Daddy
#1

Enjoy!

Mary Jacobs

2021

BIG DADDY RACCOON
AND THE BIG SECRET

Mary T. Jacobs

SkyLightBooks

An imprint of Tandem Light Press

SkyLight Books
An imprint of Tandem Light Press
950 Herrington Road
Suite C128
Lawrenceville, GA 30044

Tandem Light Press hard cover edition October 2016

ISBN: 978-0-9976797-1-7
Library of Congress Control Number: 2016956114

PRINTED IN THE UNITED STATES OF AMERICA

This book is dedicated to my
wonderful grandchildren.

They inspired me to write this book.

Acknowledgments

I would like to acknowledge several individuals that have inspired to write this book. First, I wish to acknowledge my husband, Rudy, for more than forty wonderful years. His unconditional love and encouragement continues to amaze me!

I want to express my thanks and gratitude to my editor, Caroline Donahue. She listened and encouraged me along the way as well as editing. I know future projects will be just as delightful!

And finally to my publisher, Dr. Pamela Antoinette Larde of Skylight Books, for helping me achieve a lifelong goal of publishing a children's book. I look forward to working with you again on future projects.

Once upon a time, there was an enormous, old, and wise raccoon named "Big Daddy." He roamed all over the island, but called a tree branch at an adorable yellow house near a lagoon and marsh his home.

He chose this spot because it met all his needs; which included water and food from the marsh, a spot high up in a tree for his safety, and most of all, the view to the family that lived in the yellow house. Each evening, he would sit on the tree branch and watch the family inside. And of course, they enjoyed watching him as well.

Over the years, Big Daddy noticed that each summer three children always came to visit for two weeks. They were cousins visiting their grandparents who owned the yellow house. One girl had long red hair and was named Sally, another girl had short red hair and was named Sara, and the boy, Bucky, was the youngest. He had lots of curls and loved animals. In fact, all the cousins loved animals and especially loved each other.

After about three years, something happened and Big Daddy realized that he had watched and listened to the cousins so often that he had learned how to understand what they were saying to each other. Oh, my he thought, I am now bi-lingual!

"I speak raccoon and English," he said out loud.

He realized he had a problem: who would he talk to and who would believe him?

One day, Sally was sitting on the porch reading a book about fashion. She felt like something was looking at her. To her surprise, she looked over at the tree and Big Daddy was looking back at her. She was a bit startled, because rarely did raccoons come out during the day. She was even more surprised when Big Daddy said, "How are you today?"

Sally sat and did not speak for fear of what to say. Was this real? After a few minutes that felt like days, she finally got the courage to speak.

"I'm fine, but how did you do that? Talking..." she trailed off, "Raccoons don't talk."

Big Daddy chuckled and said, "When you watch and listen, you can learn just about anything."

Big Daddy jumped from his tree limb over to the porch to get closer to Sally. He started telling her that he had learned to trust her over the years, along with her other two cousins, and he wanted to be their friend. This was to be a very special friendship because most humans would not understand that a raccoon could talk to humans.

"It is quite easy to be your friend when I see the delight in your eyes and notice the kind deeds you do for all my other friends," declared Big Daddy.

Sally smiled and said, "You're so kind to notice that about us."

Big Daddy told Sally that they should let the other two cousins, Sara and Bucky, in on the secret as well. Sally was unsure how to go about telling them, so she asked Big Daddy.

"First, we'll need to set a location. I suggest it be near the water, maybe over at the crabbing dock," smiled Big Daddy hopefully.

He explained that he knew this was where Sara and Bucky always liked to play so they could fish and catch crabs.

"Wow, you do know a lot about us," said Sally.

"Sure I do! Raccoons are naturally curious," responded Big Daddy.

"What else shall we do to be ready for the first meeting?" asked Sally.

Big Daddy, replied immediately and said, "You need to tell them that y'all need to go for a walk to the crabbing dock and take some crab nets just in case they want to do a little crabbing."

"The next thing you need to tell them is to bring a snack, perhaps something like chicken wings, biscuits, and cheese." Big Daddy smiled as he suggested the snacks. Big Daddy loved homemade biscuits.

Sally, who loved fruits and veggies, said, "Really Big Daddy, do you think that's very healthy?"

"Well, okay," said Big Daddy, "then bring fruits and veggies as well."

Sally grinned and said, "Now that's better."

The day of the introduction came. Sally carefully packed the snacks and included all the items: chicken wings, cheese, biscuits, and fruits and veggies. She carefully wrapped them in a basket to carry on her bike. She had already shared the news of the trip with Sara and Bucky, who had packed their bikes with crab nets and their fishing poles. So, off the three rode on their bikes to the crabbing dock! As they approached the dock, Sara said, "Stop! I think I see a deer that looks hungry!"

They all stopped and agreed to feed the deer some veggies. Satisfied, they then continued the trip.

Almost at the dock, Bucky yelled, "Stop! I see an alligator that needs some chicken wings."

Sally, being the oldest and the rule follower said, "Oh, no! We do NOT feed alligators! It's not safe!"

Sara agreed with Sally, and the trip continued.

Please don't feed the alligators

As they reached the crabbing dock, they noticed their grandfather. He was wearing his favorite ball cap and t-shirt with a big marlin on the back. He turned and greeted them, like he knew they were coming.

Sally was concerned that because their grandfather was there, Big Daddy wouldn't want to be introduced to her cousins. But then she remembered that her grandmother had always taught her to have a backup plan as well as be honest. So she thought quickly in case Big Daddy decided not to talk.

The cousins walked over to their grandfather who was sitting on a chair at the middle of the dock. Beside him sat Big Daddy eating on an oyster that he had just pulled out of the marsh!

They all screamed!

Sally screamed because she was supposed to have a secret and Bucky and Sara screamed because they couldn't believe their eyes.

Big Daddy smiled, "Well it's about time you guys got here with the snacks! I'm just about done with this oyster."

Sally exclaimed, "I thought no one knew you could talk but me!"

Grandfather smiled up at Sally, "Big Daddy and I have been sittin' here chatting for a while. I was pretty surprised when he shared his secret with me."

As they all sat and snacked, Sally began to understand that only a few people in this world ever slow down enough to listen to nature and learn to communicate with animals.

As they crabbed and fished, Big Daddy noticed Grandfather sneaking some biscuits, "Man oh man, Grandfather loves him some biscuits!"

"That is not proper English, Big Daddy," chided Sara.

Big Daddy smiled, "Well, I speak raccoon and English and sometimes my English isn't correct, but I promise to try and do better."

After a great trip to the crabbing dock they all agreed they would do this daily when the children visited for the summer.

Sara and Bucky wanted to know if they could meet other animal friends.

Big Daddy replied, "You already know them. Just listen as we return to the yellow house we call home

For many, many years, the children have continued to make many friends—both animal and human—in the "low country" and on beautiful Fripp Island.

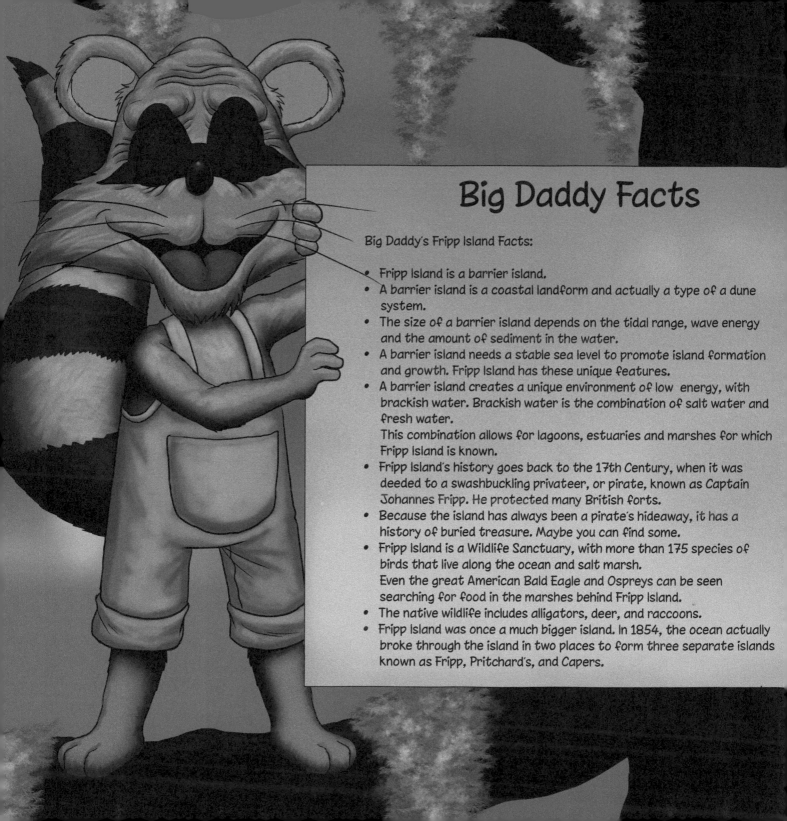

Big Daddy Facts

Big Daddy's Fripp Island Facts:

- Fripp Island is a barrier island.
- A barrier island is a coastal landform and actually a type of a dune system.
- The size of a barrier island depends on the tidal range, wave energy and the amount of sediment in the water.
- A barrier island needs a stable sea level to promote island formation and growth. Fripp Island has these unique features.
- A barrier island creates a unique environment of low energy, with brackish water. Brackish water is the combination of salt water and fresh water.
  This combination allows for lagoons, estuaries and marshes for which Fripp Island is known.
- Fripp Island's history goes back to the 17th Century, when it was deeded to a swashbuckling privateer, or pirate, known as Captain Johannes Fripp. He protected many British forts.
- Because the island has always been a pirate's hideaway, it has a history of buried treasure. Maybe you can find some.
- Fripp Island is a Wildlife Sanctuary, with more than 175 species of birds that live along the ocean and salt marsh.
  Even the great American Bald Eagle and Ospreys can be seen searching for food in the marshes behind Fripp Island.
- The native wildlife includes alligators, deer, and raccoons.
- Fripp Island was once a much bigger island. In 1854, the ocean actually broke through the island in two places to form three separate islands known as Fripp, Pritchard's, and Capers.

About the Author

Mary T. Jacobs was born in Washington, Georgia. She has been an educator for over forty years. Dr. Jacobs has published articles and her recent book entitled, Inspiring Future Leaders Through Mentoring and Coaching was released in January 2015.

Since 1999, Dr. Jacobs has served as a professor at Mercer University. Currently, Dr. Jacobs is a private consultant and serves as a consultant for Georgia State University. Dr. Jacobs has recently moved to Fripp Island, South Carolina.

CPSIA information can be obtained
at www.ICGtesting.com
Printed in the USA
BVHW020341300621
610760BV00002B/3